Mason and His Superpower

This Book belongs to

Name :

D1411307

....

Address :

....

....

First paperback edition December 2021

Cover art by Endy Astiko
Layout by Endy Astiko

Serenity Life Fitness Inc.
6615 Grand Avenue
#1009
Gurnee, IL 60099

Dedicated to all the children who have yet to discover their "Superpower"

"Wake up Mason. It's time for school," his mom called. Mason peeled himself out of bed, slowly removing the covers off his tall slender body. "School," Mason thought. "I HATE school. I don't even understand why I have to go in the first place," he grumbled.

Mason had quickly learned though that going to school wasn't an option in his home. His family believed in education. He knew that if he decided to skip school, he would have to suffer the consequences when he got home.

"Wassup bruh," hissed Tyreek as Mason slithered into his seat. Tyreek was in Mason's homeroom class. He was also one of the most popular athletes in school and a star player on Lincoln Tech's Basketball Team. In fact, he was magical with any sport he played. Athleticism was his superpower. "Wassup man," said Mason.

"Alright class, settle down and open up your agendas," Mrs. Henry yelled to the class. Immediately, Mason's mind began to drift off. Mason's dad always wanted him to play sports. "Athleticism is in your blood son," Mason could hear his father say. Even though playing sports was fun, it just wasn't Mason's thing. He had tried wrestling, basketball, boxing, football, and even track. BUT he just couldn't muster up the motivation to continue with sports.

"Hey Mason," Jessica said as she nudged Mason's shoulder. "Are you even paying attention?" "Uh nope!" Mason quickly retorted. They both burst into laughter. "What's so funny guys," asked Mrs. Henry. "Unless you are willing to share with the entire class what you two find so funny, I suggest you turn around and be quiet." Jessica rolled her eyes at Mrs. Henry, but quickly gave in to her teacher's request. Even though Jessica loved to laugh with her friends in class, she was still at the top of her class.

She had a 4.0 GPA, and the teachers always praised her for her remarkable grades. Performing well in school was her superpower. But that wasn't the case for Mason.

You see, Mason was just a typical boy. He was okay with being average. When his parents would talk about how GREAT they thought he was, he just tuned them out. It wasn't that he didn't want to hear that he had potential, he just hadn't discovered what made him extraordinary. While it seemed like everyone else around him quickly discovered their talent, Mason was stuck.

The next day, Mason went to school prepared to daydream as he typically did in class. "Good morning class. Today, I want you to write about your superpower. In other words, I want you to think about what you are really good at. You will write about it, and then present it to the class," announced Mrs. Henry. "Oh great," thought Mason. "I have no idea what I'm going to write about. Maybe, I can just copy off Jason's paper so I can get this stupid assignment done." As Mrs. Henry continued to explain the assignment, she handed out a worksheet with "My Superpower is" in the middle and a web around it. "Class, I want you to use this worksheet to brainstorm ideas. This will help you put your thoughts on paper," said Mrs. Henry. Mason was clueless and decided it would be a good time to take a nap.

"Psst. Psst. Mason!" Jessica quietly whispered. When Mason didn't wake up, she decided to pinch his arm. "Owwww," yelled Mason, loud enough for the entire class to hear. The class began to laugh in an uproar.

"Mason, what seems to be the problem now?" Mrs. Henry asked with that stern momma look teachers give when they mean business. "Oh nothing, I'm cool," replied Mason. "Well, get to work and stop trying to disrupt my class," demanded Mrs. Henry.

Read Me!

"Riinnnnnnng!!" The bell rang just in time for class to be dismissed. "Whew, thank God," Mason thought. On the way out of class, Mrs. Henry reminded them of their homework and told them they must complete the SuperPower Brainstorming Worksheet by tomorrow. Mason quickly grabbed his book bag and headed out the door, when he noticed a piece of paper slipped from his desk onto the floor. It was folded up neatly and on the top said, "Read Me!"

Mason quickly picked up the paper and rushed out of class. He let the entire school day pass before he thought to read the note. When he was finally home and in his room, he unraveled the note:

Mason, your Superpower is that you are funny and can always make me laugh when I am having a bad day. Write about that!
Signed,
Jessica

Suddenly, Mason's eyes got big and wide. He thought about all the times at home when his sister was sad, and he would tell jokes to lighten her mood. He also thought about the days that his dad would argue with him about his grades, and he would eventually find a way to make his dad laugh. He even thought about all the times his friends would come to him and tell him all their problems, not for advice, but because they knew that Mason would find a way to make their problems seem small.

The next day, Mason walked into Mrs. Henry's class with a smile on his face. At least he knew that if he had done nothing for the other classes, he could turn in one assignment. "Ah ah ah, where's your homework,"asked Mrs. Henry as Mason was walking past her desk. "Oh yeah," said Mason as he took out the wrinkled worksheet and handed it to his teacher. In the middle of the paper, it read, "Making People Laugh is my Superpower". Mrs. Henry smiled back at him and nodded her head in agreement. Mason thought, "I think I can make it through this class after all." As he headed back to his seat, he winked at Jessica and whispered, "Thank you."

Author Page

Natoia Franklin is an educator, Holistic Health Coach, personal trainer, and group fitness extraordinaire for women and children. As the owner of Serenity Life Fitness and co-founder of RHYTHM Academy, she offers services that inspire physical, mental, and spiritual transformation. She is passionate about serving underserved communities while ensuring that those communities get access and exposure to effective wellness programs that target obesity, poor nutrition, mental health issues, and sedentary lifestyles. When she is not training or teaching, she is busy being a mom to her four children and wife to her husband. Website: www.serenitylifefitness.com

Made in the USA
Middletown, DE
11 May 2022

65610142R00015

Mason and His Superpower

Mason is a typical 7th grader who hates school. School is boring, and he can't seem to focus in class. Everyone else around him has discovered what they are really good at except him. One day he is asked by Mrs. Henry to complete an assignment that challenges him to figure out his talent. With help from his family and friends, Mason finally finds his Superpower.

ISBN 9780578351308

9 780578 351308

O9-ADD-742